**Adam Mickiewicz**

# Konrad Wallenrod

# Adam Mickiewicz

# Konrad Wallenrod

1. Auflage | ISBN: 978-3-75243-898-7

Erscheinungsort: Frankfurt am Main, Deutschland

Erscheinungsjahr: 2020

Outlook Verlag GmbH, Deutschland.

# KONRAD WALLENROD.

## An Historical Poem.

BY

ADAM MICKIEWICZ.

# AUTHOR'S PREFACE

THE Lithuanian nation, formed out of the tribes of the Litwini, Prussians and Leti, not very numerous, settled in an inextensive country, not very fertile, long unknown to Europe, was called, about the thirteenth century, by the incursions of its neighbours, to a more active part. When the Prussians submitted to the swords of the Teutonic knights, the Lithuanians, issuing from their forests and marshes, annihilated with sword and fire the neighbouring empires, and soon became terrible in the north. History has not as yet satisfactorily explained by what means a nation so weak, and so long tributary to foreigners, was able all at once to oppose and threaten all its enemies—on one side, carrying on a constant and murderous war with the Teutonic Order; on the other, plundering Poland, exacting tribute from Great Novgorod, and pushing itself as far as the borders of the Wolga and the Crimean peninsula. The brightest period of Lithuanian [pg iv] history occurs in the time of Olgierd and Witold, whose rule extended from the Baltic to the Black Sea. But this monstrous empire, having sprung up too quickly, could not create in itself internal strength, to unite and invigorate its differing portions. The Lithuanian nationality, spread over too large a surface of territory, lost its proper character. The Litwini subjugated many Russian tribes, and entered into political relations with Poland. The Slavs, long since Christians, stood in a higher degree of civilisation, and although conquered, or threatened by Lithuania, gained by gradual influence a moral preponderance over their strong, but barbarous tyrants, and absorbed them, as the Chinese their Tartar invaders. The Jagellons, and their more powerful vassals, became Poles; many Lithuanian princes adopted the Russian religion, language, and nationality. By these means the Grand Duchy of Lithuania ceased to be Lithuanian; the nation proper found itself within its former boundaries, its speech ceased to be the language of the court and nobility, and was only preserved among the common people. Litwa presents the singular spectacle of a people which disappeared in the immensity of its conquests, as a brook sinks after an excessive overflow, and flows in a narrower bed than before.

[pg v]

The circumstances here mentioned are covered by some centuries. Both Lithuania, and her cruellest enemy, the Teutonic Order, have disappeared from the scene of political life; the relations between neighbouring nations are entirely changed; the interests and passions which kindled the wars of that time are now expired; even popular song has not preserved their memory. Litwa is now entirely in the past: her history presents from this circumstance a happy theme for poetry; so that a poet, in singing of the events of that time, objects only of historic interest, must occupy himself with searching into, and with artfully rendering the subject, without summoning to his aid the interests, passions, or fashions of his readers. For such subjects Schiller recommended poets to seek.

"Was unsterblich im Gesang will leben,

Muss im Leben untergehen."

---

[pg vii]

# TRANSLATOR'S PREFACE

The Teutonic Order, originally, like the Knights Hospitallers, established in the Holy Land about 1199, settled, after the cessation of the Crusades, in the country bordering upon the Baltic Sea, at the mouth of the Vistula, in the year 1225. The possession of the Baltic shores, and of such lands as the Order should conquer from the pagan Prussians and Litwini, was assured to them by Konrad, Duke of Masowsze, brother to Leszek the White of Poland. The fatal error thus committed, in abandoning a hold on the sea-coast, had afterwards a disastrous effect on the history of Poland. The Order speedily made themselves masters of the whole country of Prussia, and were engaged in ceaseless war with the pagans of Lithuania, under pretext of their conversion; more frequently, it is however to be feared, for purposes of raid and plunder. It is, in fact, upon record that a certain Lithuanian prince, who had [pg viii] offered to embrace Christianity for the purpose of recovering part of his territory conquered by the Order, upon finding that his conversion would produce no better disposition in them towards himself, declared his intention of abiding in paganism, with the remark that he saw it was no question of his faith, but of his possessions. The plundering expeditions of the Teutonic knights up country, in which many of the chivalry of all Europe frequently bore a part, were termed *reyses*. The English reader will remember how Chaucer's knight had fought "aboven alle nations in Pruce."

"In *Lettow had he reysed* and in Ruce."

Henry IV. also, during his banishment, fought in the ranks of the Order.

After the conversion of Lithuania, and the union of that country with Poland, the Teutonic knights were frequently engaged in hostilities with both powers combined, sustaining in the year 1410 a terrible defeat at Tannenberg in E. Prussia, from the forces of Jagellon. In this battle it is worthy of note that the famous John Ziska was engaged. In 1466 Casimir Jagellon inflicted heavy losses on the Order. After its secularisation in 1521, when the Grand-Master Albert embraced the reformed [pg ix] faith, the domains of E. Prussia were held as a fief from Poland. In 1657 Prussia became an independent state under Frederick William, the great Elector. It is curious to observe how the name of Prussia, originally that of a conquered, non-Germanic people, has become in our time that of the first German power in the world.

The historical circumstances on which the poem of "Konrad Wallenrod" is founded are thus detailed at length by the author himself, in the following postscript to the work:—

"We have called our story historical, for the characters of the actors, and all the more important circumstances mentioned therein, are sketched according to history. The contemporary chronicles, in fragmentary and broken portions, must be filled out sometimes only by guesses and conjectures, in order to create some historic entirety from them. Although I have permitted myself conjectures in the history of Wallenrod, I hope to justify them by their likeness to truth. According to the chronicle, Konrad Wallenrod was not descended from the family of Wallenrod renowned in Germany, though he gave himself out as a member of it. He was said to have been born of some illicit connection. The royal chronicle says, 'Er war ein Pfaffenkind.' Concerning the character of this singular man, we [pg x] read many and contradictory traditions. The greater number of the chroniclers reproach him with pride, cruelty, drunkenness, severity towards his subordinates, little zeal for religion, and even with hatred for ecclesiastics. 'Er war ein rechter Leuteschinder (library of Wallenrod). Nach Krieg, Zank, und Hader hat sein Herz immer gestanden; und ob er gleich ein Gott ergebener Mensch von wegen seines Ordens sein wollte, doch ist er allen frommen geistlichen Menschen Graüel gewesen. (David Lucas). Er regierte nicht lange, denn Gott plagte ihn inwendig mit dem laufenden Feuer.' On the other hand, contemporary writers ascribe to him greatness of intellect, courage, nobility, and force of character; since without rare qualities he could not have maintained his empire amid universal hatred and the disasters which he brought upon the Order. Let us now consider the proceedings of Wallenrod. When he assumed the rule of the Order, the season appeared favourable for war with Lithuania, for Witold had promised himself to lead the Germans to Wilna, and liberally repay them for their assistance. Wallenrod, however, delayed to go to war; and, what was worse, offended Witold, and reposed such careless confidence in him, that this prince, having secretly become reconciled to Jagellon, not only departed from Prussia, but on [pg xi] the road, entering the German castles, burnt them as an enemy, and slaughtered the garrisons. In such an unimagined change of circumstances, it was needful to neglect the war, or undertake it with great prudence. The Grand-Master proclaimed a crusade, wasted the treasures of the Order in preparation—5,000,000 marks—a sum at that time immeasurable, and marched towards Lithuania. He could have captured Wilna, if he had not wasted time in banquets and waiting for auxiliaries. Autumn came; Wallenrod, leaving the camp without provisions, retired in the greatest disorder to Prussia. The chroniclers and later historians were not able to imagine the cause of this sudden departure, not finding in contemporary circumstances any cause therefor. Some have assigned the flight of Wallenrod to derangement of intellect. All the contradictions mentioned in the character and conduct of our hero may be reconciled with each other, if we suppose that he was a Lithuanian, and that he had entered the Order to take vengeance on it; especially since his rule gave the severest shock to the power of the Order. We suppose that Wallenrod was Walter Stadion (see note), shortening only by some years the time which passed between the departure of Walter from Lithuania, and the appearance of [pg xii] Konrad in Marienbourg. Wallenrod died suddenly in the year 1394; strange events were said to have accompanied his death. 'Er starb,' says the chronicle; 'in Raserei ohne letzte Oehlung, ohne Priestersegen, kurz vor seinem Tode wütheten Stürme, Regensgüsse, Wasserfluthen; die Weichsel und die Nogat durchwühlten ihre Dämme; hingegen wühlten die gewässer sich eine neue Tiefe da, wo jetzt Pilau steht!' Halban, or, as the chroniclers call him, Doctor Leander von Albanus, a monk, the solitary and inseparable companion of Wallenrod, though he assumed the appearance of piety, was according to the chroniclers a heretic, a pagan, and perhaps a wizard. Concerning Halban's death, there are no certain accounts. Some write that he was drowned, others that he disappeared secretly, or was carried away by demons. I have drawn the chronicles chiefly from the works of Kotzebue, 'Preussens Geschichte, Belege und Erläuterungen.' Hartknoch, in calling Wallenrod 'unsinnig,' gives a very short account of him."

As to the conditions under which the poem was written, it is perhaps needful to state that it was composed by Mickiewicz, during the term of his banishment into Russia, and was first published at St. Petersburg in the year 1828. In the character of [pg xiii] the hero of the story, and in various circumstances of the poem, it is impossible not to recognise the influence of Lord Byron's poetry, which obtained so powerful an ascendency over the works and imaginations of the Continental romanticists, and had thus an influence over foreign literature not conceded in the poet's own country. The Byronic character, however, presents a far nobler aspect in the hands of the present author than in those of its original creator; for, instead of being the outcome of a mere morbid self-concentration, and brooding over personal wrongs, it is the result of a noble indignation for the sufferings of others, and is conjoined with a high purpose for good, even though such good be worked out by means in themselves doubtful or questionable.

We cannot pass by the subject without saying a word as to the undercurrent of political meaning in "Konrad Wallenrod," which fortunately escaped the rigid censorship of the Russian press. Lithuania, conquered and oppressed by the Teutonic Order, is Poland, subjugated by Russia; and the numerous expressions of hatred for oppressors and love of an unhappy country woven into the substance of the narrative must be read as the utterances of a Pole against Russian tyranny. The underhand machinations of the concealed enemy [pg xiv] against the state in which he is a powerful leader, may be held to figure that intricate web of intrigue and conspiracy which Russian liberalism is gradually weaving throughout the whole political system, and which is daily gaining influence and power. The character of Wallenrod is essentially the same as that of Cooper's "Spy;" but we cannot suppose that the author intended to hold up trickery and deceit as praiseworthy and honourable, even though it is the sad necessity of slaves to use treachery as their only weapon; or that the Macchiavellian precept with which the story is headed is at all intended as one to be generally followed by seekers of political liberty against despotism. The end and aim of this, as of all the works of Mickiewicz, is to show us a great and noble soul, noble in spite of many errors and vices, striving to work out a high ideal, and the fulfilment of a noble purpose; and to exhibit the heroism of renunciation of personal ease and enjoyment for the sake of the world's or a nation's good.

In regard to the method used in the English version, it is only necessary to add that as far as possible verbal accuracy in rendering has been endeavoured after; and an attempt, at least conscientious—whether or not partially successful must be left to the sentence of those qualified to [pg xv] form an opinion—has been made to reproduce as nearly as may be something of the original spirit In translating the main body of the narrative blank verse has been the medium employed, not as at all representing the beautiful and harmonious interchange of rhymes and play of rhythm so conspicuous in the Polish lines; but as securing, by reason of freedom from the necessity for rhymes, a truer verbal rendering, and as being the measure par excellence best suited to English narrative verse. The "Wajdelote's Tale" has for similar reasons been rendered into the same form, instead of being reproduced in the original hexameter stanza, as strange to the Polish as to the English tongue, wherein, despite the works of Longfellow and Clough, it can hardly be said to have yet become thoroughly naturalised. Most of the lyrics are translated into the same metres as the originals, with the sole exception of the ballad of Alpujara. This, as being upon a Spanish or Moorish subject, it was judged best to render into a form nearly resembling that of the ancient Spanish ballad, and employed by Bishop Percy in translation of the "Rio Verde," and other poems from a like source. Moreover, the original "Alpujara" is couched in a metre which, though extremely well suited to the Polish tongue, is difficult [pg xvi] of imitation in English; or only to be imitated by great loss of accuracy in rendering.

In concluding, the translator begs to express a hope that this humble effort to present, however feebly, to the reading public of Great Britain an image of the work of the greatest of Polish poets, may, not be wholly unacceptable. Any defects which the critical eye may note, must undoubtedly be laid rather to the charge of the copyist, than to the original of the great master. I dare, however, to trust, that the shadow of so great a name, and the sincere wish to contribute this slender homage to the memory of one of Europe's most illustrious writers, may serve as an excuse for over-presumption.

LONDON, *March* 1882.

# Introduction.

A HUNDRED years have passed since first the Order
Waded in blood of Northern heathenesse;
The Prussian now had bent his neck to chains,
Or, yielding up his heritage, removed
With life alone. The German followed after,
Tracking the fugitive; he captive made
And murdered unto Litwa's farthest bound.
Niemen divideth Litwa from the foe;
On one side gleam the sanctuary fanes,
And forests murmur, dwellings of the gods.
[pg 2]
Upon the other shore the German ensign,
The cross, implanted on a hill, doth veil
Its forehead in the clouds, and stretches forth

Its threatening arms towards Litwa, as it would
Gather all lands of Palemon together,
Embrace them all, assembled 'neath its rule.
This side, the multitude of Litwa's youth,
With *kolpak* of the lynx-hide and in skins
Clad of the bear, the bow upon their shoulders,
Their hands all filled with darts, they prowl around,
Tracking the German wiles. On the other side,
In mail and helmet armed, the German sits
Upon his charger motionless; while fixed
His eyes upon the entrenchments of the foe,
He loads his arquebuse and counts his beads.
And these and those alike the passageguard.
The Niemen thus, of hospitable fame,
In ancient days, uniting heritage
Of brother nations, now for thembecomes
The threshold of eternity, and none,
But by foregoing liberty or life,
Cross the forbidden waters. Only now
A trailer of the Lithuanian hop,
[pg 3]
Drawn by allurement of the Prussian poplar,
Stretches its fearless arms, as formerly,
Leaping the river, with luxuriant wreaths,
Twines with its loved one on a foreign shore.
The nightingales from Kowno's groves of oak
Still with their brethren of Zapuszczan mount,
Converse, as once, in Lithuanian speech.
Or having on free pinions 'scaped, they fly,

As guests familiar, on the neutral isles.
And mankind?—War has severed human kind!
The ancient love of nations has departed
Into oblivion. Love by time alone
Uniteth human hearts.—Two hearts I knew.
O Niemen! soon upon thy fords shall rush
Hosts bearing death and burning, and thy shores,
Sacred till now, the axe shall render bare
Of all their garlands; soon the cannon's roar
Shall from the gardens fright the nightingales.
Where nature with a golden chain hath bound,
The hatred of the nations shall divide;
It severs all things. But the hearts of lovers
Shall in the Wajdelote's song unite once more.

---

[pg 4]

# The Election.

In towers of Marienbourg[1] the bells are ringing,
The cannon thunder loud, the drums are beating.
This in the Order is a solemn day.
The Komturs hasten to the capital,

Where, gathered in the chapter's conclave, they,
The Holy Spirit invoked, take counsel who
Is worthiest to bear the mighty sword,—
Into whose hands may they confide the sword?
One day, and yet another flowed away
In council; many heroes there contend.
And all alike of noble race, and all
Alike deserving in the Order's cause.
But hitherto the brethren's general voice
Placed Wallenrod the highest over all
A stranger he, in Prussia all unknown,
But foreign houses of his fame werefull[2]
Following the Moors upon Castilian sierras,
The Ottoman through ocean's troubled waves,
In battle at the front, first on the wall,
To grapple vessels of the infidel
The first; and in the tourney, soon as he
Entered the lists and deigned his visor raise,
[pg 5]
None dared with him the strife of keen-edged swords,[3]
By one accord the victor's garland yielding.
But not alone amid Crusading hosts
He with the sword had glorified his youth;
For many Christian graces him adorn,
Poverty, humbleness, of earth disdain.
But Konrad shone not in the courtly crowd
By polished speech, by well-turned reverence;
Nor e'er his sword for vile advantage sold
To service of disputing barons. He

Had consecrated to the cloister walls
His youthful years; all plaudits he disdained,
And ruler's place, even higher, sweeter meeds.
Nor minstrel's hymn, nor beauty's fair regard
Could speak to his cold spirit. Wallenrod
Listens unmoved to praise, and looks afar
On lovely cheeks, enchanting discourse flies.
Had Nature made him thus unfeeling, proud?
Or age? For albeit young in years, his locks
Were grey already, withered were his looks,
And sufferings sealed by age.—Twere hard to guess.
He would at times divide the sports of youth,
[pg 6]
Or listen, pleased, to sound of female tongues,
To courtiers' jests reply with other jests;
Or scatter unto ladies courteous words
With chilly smile, as dainties cast to children—
These were rare moments of forgetfulness;—
And speedily some light, unmeaning word,
That had no sense for others, woke in him
Passionate stirrings. These words: Fatherland,
Duty, Beloved,—the mention of Crusades,
And Litwa, all the mirth of Wallenrod
Instantly poisoned. Hearing them, again
He turned away his countenance, again
Became to all around insensible,
And buried him in thoughts mysterious.
Maybe, remembering his holy call,
He would forbid himself the sweets of earth;

The sweets of friendship only did heknow,
One only friend had chosen to himself,
A saint by virtue and by holy state.
This was a hoary monk; men called him Halban.
He shared the loneliness of Wallenrod;
He was alike confessor of his soul,
And of his heart the trusted confidant
O blessed friendship! saint is he on earth,
Whom friendship with the holy ones unites.
[pg 7]
Thus do the leaders of the Order's council
Discourse of Konrad's virtues. But one fault
Was his,—for who may spotless be from faults?
Konrad loved not the riots of the world,
Nor mingled Konrad in the drunken feast.
Though truly, in his secret chamber locked,
When weariness or sorrow tortured him,
He sought for solace in a burning draught;
And then he seemed a new form to indue,
And then his visage pallid and severe
A sickly red adorned, and his large eyes,
Erst heavenly blue, but somewhat now by time
Dulled and extinguished, shot the lightnings forth
Of ancient fires, while sighs of grief escape
From forth his breast, and with the pearly tear
The laden eyelid swells; the hand the lute
Seeks, the lips pour forth songs; the songs are sung
In speech of a strange land, but yet the hearts
Of the hearers understand them. 'Tis enough

To list that grave-like music, 'tis enough
The singer's form to contemplate, to see
Memory's inspiration on that face,
To view the lifted brows and sideward looks,
Striving to snatch some object from deep darkness.
What may the hidden thread be of the songs?
[pg 8]
He tracketh surely, in this wandering chase,
In thought his youth through deep gulfs of the past.
Where is his soul?—In the land of memories!
But never did that hand in music's impulse
Mere joyful tones from out the lute evoke;
And still it seemed his countenance did fear
Innocent smiles, even as deadly sins.
All strings he strikes in turn, one string except—
Except the string of mirth;—the hearer shares
All feelings with him,—one excepted—hope!
Not seldom him the brethren have surprised,
And marvelled at his unaccustomed change.
Konrad, aroused, did writhe himself and rage,
Had cast away the lute and ceased to sing.
He spoke out loudly impious words; to Halban
Whispered some secret things; called to the host,
Gave forth commands, and uttered dreadful threats,
On whom they knew not. All their hearts were troubled.
Old Halban tranquil sits, and on the face
Of Konrad drowns his glance,—a piercing glance,
Cold and severe, full of some secret speech.
[pg 9]

Something he may recall, some counsel give,
Or waken grief in heart of Wallenrod,
Whose cloudy brow at once is calm again,
His eyes forego their fires, his rage is cool.
Thus when, in public sport, the lionward,
Before assembled lords, and dames, and knights,
Unbars the grating of the iron cage.
The trumpet signal given, the royal beast
Growls from his deep breast, horror falls on all.
Alone his keeper moveth not a step,
Folds tranquilly upon his breast his hands,
And smites with power the lion,—by the eye.
With talisman of an undying soul
Unreasoning strength in bonds he doth control.
[pg 10]

# II.

In towers of Marienbourg the bells are ringing;
Now from the hall of council to the chapel
Comes the chief Komtur, then the chiefest rulers,
The chaplain, brothers, and assembled knights.
The chapter listen vesper orisons,
And sing a hymn unto the Holy Spirit

HYMN.

Spirit! Thou Holy One,
Thou Dove of Sion's Hill!

This Christian world, the footstool of Thy throne,
With glory visible
Lighten, that all behold.
Thy wings o'er Sion's brotherhood unfold,
And let Thy glory shine from underneath
Thy wings, with sunlike rays.
[pg 11]
And him, the worthiest of so holy praise,
Circle his temples with Thy golden wreath.
Fall on the visage of that son of man,
Whom shadows o'er Thy wings' protecting van.
Thou Saviour Son!
With beckoning of Thy hand almighty, deign
To point of many one,
Worthiest to hold,
And wear the sacred symbol of Thy pain.
To lead with Peter's sword thy soldiery,
Before the eyes of heathenesse unfold
The standards of Thy heavenly empery.
Then let the sons of earth bow lowly down,
Him on whose breast the cross shall gleam to own.

Prayers o'er, they parted. The Archkomtur[4] ordered
After repose, to seek the choir again;
Again entreat that Heaven would enlighten
Chaplains and brethren, called to such election.
So went they forth themselves to recreate
With the cool freshness of the night; and some
Sat in the castle porch, and others walk
[pg 12]

Through gardens and through groves. The night was still;
It was the fair May season; from afar
Peeped forth the pale uncertain dawn; the moon,
Having the sapphire plains o'ercoursed, with aspect
Changing, with varying lustre in her eye,
Now in a shadowy, now a silvery cloud
Slumbering, now sank her still and tranquil head,
Like to a lover in the wilderness;
Dreaming in thought, life's circle heo'erruns,
All hopes, all sweetness, and all sufferings.
Now sheds he tears, now joyful is his glance.
At length upon his breast the weary brow
Sinketh, and falls in sense's lethargy.
By walking other knights beguile the time,
But the Archkomtur wastes no time in vain.
He quickly summons Halban and the chiefs
Unto himself, and leads them to one side;
That, from the curious crowd afar removed,
They may pursue their counsels and impart
Forewarnings; from the castle go they forth.
They hasten to the plain. Conversing thus,
All heedless of their path, some hours astray
They wandered in the region close beside
[pg 13]
The inlets of a tranquil lake. 'Tis morn!
This hour they should regain the capital.
They stop,—a voice,—whence? From the corner tower!
They listen,—'tis the voice of the recluse!
Long time within this tower, ten summers since,

Some unknown pious woman, from afar,[5]
Who came to Mary's town,—Maybe that Heaven
Inspired her blest design, or with the balm
Of penance she would heal the wounds of conscience,—
Did seek the shelter of a lone recluse,
And here she found while living yet a tomb.
Long time the chaplains would not give consent.
Then, wearied by the constancy of prayers,
They gave her in this tower a shelter lone.
Scarcely the sacred threshold had she crossed,
When o'er the threshold bricks and stones were piled;
The angels only, in the judgment-day
Shall ope the door which parts her from the living.
Above a little window and a grate,
Whereby the pious folk send nourishment,
[pg 14]
And Heaven sends breezes and the rays of day.
Poor sinner! was it hatred of the world
Abused thy young heart to so great extreme
That thou dost fear the sun. and heaven's fair face?
Scarcely imprisoned in her living grave,
None saw her, through the window of the tower,
Receive upon her lips the wind's fresh breath,
Nor look upon the heaven in sunshine beauty,
Or the sweet flowerets on the plain of earth,
Or, dearer hundred-fold, her fellow-men.
'Tis only known that still she is in life;
For when betimes a holy pilgrim wanders
Near her retreat by night, a sweet, low sound

Holds him awhile. Certain it is the sound
Of pious hymns. And when the village children
Together in the oak-grove sport at eve,
Then from the window shines a streak of white,
As 'twere a sunbeam from the rising dawn.
Is it an amber ringlet of her hair,
Or lustre of her slender, snowy hand
Blessing those innocent heads? The chivalry
Hear as they pass the corner tower these words:
"Thou art Konrad! Heaven! Fate is now fulfilled!
[pg 15]
Thou shalt be Master, that thou mayest destroy them!
Will they not recognise?—Thou hid'st in vain.
Though like the serpent's were thy body changed,
Yet of the past would in thy soul remain
Many things still,—truly they cleave to me.
Though after burial thou shouldst return,
Then, even then, would the Crusaders know thee!"
The knights attend,—'tis the recluse's voice;
They look upon the grate; she bending seems,
Towards the earth she seems her arms to stretch.
To whom? The region is all desert round;
Only from far strikes an uncertain gleam,
In likeness of a steely helmet's flame,
A shadow on the earth, a knightly cloak;—
Already it has vanished. Certainly
'Twas an illusion of the eyes, most certain
It was the rosy glance of morn that gleamed.
For morning's clouds now rolled away from earth.

"Brothers!" spoke Halban, "give we thanks to Heaven,
For certain Heaven's decree hath led us here;
Trust we to the recluse's prophet voice.
[pg 16]
Heard ye? She made a prophecy of Konrad,—
Konrad, the name of valiant Wallenrod!
Let brother unto brother give the hand,
And knightly word, and in to-morrow's council
Our Master he!"[6]—"Agreed," they cried, "agreed!"
And shouting went they. Far along the vale
Resounds the voice of triumph and of joy;
"Long Konrad live! long the Grand-Master live!
Long live the Order! perish heathenesse!"
Halban remained behind, in deep thought plunged;
He on the shouters cast an eye of scorn
He looked towards the tower, and in low tones,
This song he sang, departing from the place:—

Song.

Wilija, thou parent of streams in our land,
Heaven-blue is thy visage and golden thy sand;
But, lovely Litwinka,[J] who drinkest its wave,
Far purer thy heart, and thy beauty more brave.
Wilija, thou flowest through Kowno's fair vale,
Amid the gay tulips and narcissus pale.
[pg 17]
At the feet of the maiden, the flower of our youth,
Than roses, than tulips, far fairer in sooth.
The Wilija despiseth the valley of flowers,
She seeks to the Niemen, her lover, to rove;

The Litwinka listens no love-tale of ours,
The youth of the strangers has filled her with love.
In powerful embrace doth the Niemen enfold,
And beareth o'er rocks and o'er wild deserts lone;
He presses his love to his bosom so cold,
They perish together in sea-depths unknown.
Thee too, poor Litwinka, the stranger shall call
Away from the joys of that sweet native vale;
Thou deep in Forgetfulness' billows must fall,
But sadder thy fate, for alone thou must fail.
For streamlet and heart by no warning are crost,
The maiden will love and the Wilija will run;
And in her loved Niemen the Wilija is lost,
In the dark prison-tower weeps the maiden undone.

[pg 18]

# III.

When the Grand-Master had the sacred books

Kissed of the holy laws, and from the Komtur

Received the sword and grand cross, ensigns high

Of power, he raised his haughty brow. Although

A cloud of care weighed on him, with his eye

He scattered fire around him. In his glance

Burns exultation, half with anger mixed,—

And, guest invisible, upon his face

Hovered a faint and transitory smile,

Like lightning which divides the morning cloud,

Boding at once the sunrise and the thunder.

The Master's zeal, his threatening countenance,

All hearts with hope and newer courage fills;

Battle before them they behold and plunder,

And pour in thought great floods of pagan blood.

Who shall against such ruler dare to stand?

Who will not fear his sabre or his glance?

[pg 19]

Tremble, Litwini! for the time is near,

From Wilna's ramparts when the cross shall shine.

Vain are their hopes, for days and weeks flew by;

In peace a whole long year has flowed away,

And Litwa threatens. Wallenrod, ignobly

Himself nor combats, nor goes out to war;

And when he rouses and begins to act,

Reverses the old ruling suddenly.

He cries, "The Order has o'erstepped its laws,

The brethren violate their plighted vows.

Let us engage in prayer, renounce our treasures,

And seek in virtue and in peace renown."

To penance he compels them, fasts, and burdens;

Denies all pleasures, comforts innocent;

Each venial sin doth cruelly chastise

With dungeons underground, exile, the sword.

Meanwhile the Litwin, who long years afar

Had shunned the portals of the Order's town,

Now burns the villages around each night,

And captive their defenceless people takes.

Beneath the very castle proudly boasts,

He in the Master's chapel goes to mass.

[pg 20]

And children trembled on their parents' threshold,

To hear the roar of Samogitia's horn.

What time were better to begin a war

While Litwa by internal strife is torn?

Here the bold Rusin,[2] here the unquiet Lach,[3]

The Crimean Khans lead on a mighty host;

And Witold, by Jagellon dispossessed,

Has come to seek protection of the Order;

In recompense doth promise gold and land,

But hitherto for help he waits in vain.

The brothers murmur, council now assembles,

The Master is not seen. Old Halban hastes,
But in the castle, in the chapel finds
Not Konrad. Whither is he? At the tower!
The brotherhood have tracked his steps by night.
'Tis known to all; for at the evening hour,
When all the earth is veiled with thickest mists,
He sallies forth to wander by the lake.
Or on his knees, supported by the wall,
[pg 21]
Draped in his mantle, till the white dawn gleams,
He lieth, moveless as a marble form,
And unsubdued by sleep the whole nightlong.
Oft at the soft voice of the fair recluse
He rises, and returns her low replies.
No ear their import can discern afar;
But from the lustre of the shaking helm,
View of the lifted head, unquiet hands,
'Tis seen some discourse pends of weighty things.

SONG FROM THE TOWER.

Ah! who shall number all my tears and sighs?
Have I so long wept through these weary years?
Was such great bitterness in heart and eyes,
That all this grate is rusty with my tears?
Where falls the tear it penetrates the stone,
As in a good man's heart 'twere sinking down.

A fire eternal burns in Swentorog's halls;[7]
Its pious priests for ever feed the fire:
From Mendog's hill a fount eternal falls;
The snows and storm-clouds swell it ever higher.

None feed the torrent of my sighs and tears,

Yet pain for ever heart and eyeballs sears.

[pg 22]

A father's care, a mother's tender love,

And a rich castle and a joyous land,

Days without longing, nights no dream might move

Peace like a tranquil angel aye did stand

Near me, abroad, at home, by day and night,

Guarding me close, though viewless to the sight.

Three lovely daughters from one mother born,

And I the first demanded as a bride;

Happy in youth, happy in joys to be,

Who told me there were other joys beside?

O lovely youth! why didst thou tell me more

Than e'er in Litwa any knew before?

Of the great God, of angels bright as day,

Of stone-built cities where religion rests,

Where in rich churches all the people pray,

Where princely lords obey their maidens' hests;

Like to our warriors great in warlike pains,

Tender in love as are our shepherd swains.

Where man, from covering of clay set free,

A winged soul, flies through a joyful heaven.

I could believe it, for in listening thee

I had a foretaste of those wonders even.

[pg 23]

Ah! since that time, in good and evil plight,

I dream of thee and those fair heavens bright.

The cross upon thy breast rejoiced mine eyes;

The sign of future bliss therein I read.
Alas! when from the cross the thunder flies,
All things around are silenced, perished.
Nought I regret, though bitter tears I pour;
Thou tookest all from me, but hope leftst o'er.
"Hope!" the low echoes from the shore replied,
The valleys and the forest Konrad woke,
And laughing wildly, answered, "Where am I?
To hear in this place—hope? Wherefore this song?
I do recall thy vanished happiness.
Three lovely daughters from one mother born,
And thou the first demanded as a bride.
Woe unto you, fair flowers! woe to you!
A fearful viper crept into the garden,
And where the reptile's livid breast has touched
The grass is withered and the roses fade,
And yellow as the reptile's bosom grow.
Fly from the present in thought; recall the days
Which thou hadst spent in joyousness without—
[pg 24]
Thou'rt silent! Raise thy voice again and curse;
Let not the dreadful tear which pierces stones
Perish in vain. My helmet I'll remove.
Here let it fall; I am prepared to suffer;
Would learn betimes what waiteth me in hell.

VOICE FROM THE TOWER.

Pardon, my loved one, pardon! I am guilty!
Late was thy coming, weary 'twas to wait,
And thus, despite myself, some childish song—

Away with it! What have I to regret?
With thee, my love, with thee a passing space
We lived through; but the memory of that time
I would not change with all earth's habitants,
For tranquil life passed through in weariness.
Thyself didst say to me that common men
Are as those shells deep hidden in the marsh;
Scarce once a year by some tempestuous wave
Cast up, they peep from out the troubled water,
Open their lips, and sigh forth once towards heaven,
And to their burial once more return.
No! I am not created for such bliss.
While yet within my Fatherland Idwelt
[pg 25]
A still life, sometimes in my comrades' midst
A longing seized me, and I sighed in secret,
And felt unquiet throbbings in my heart;
And sometimes fled I from the lower plain,
And standing on the higher hill, I thought,
If but the larks would give me from their wings
One feather only, I would fly with them,
And only from this mountain wish to pluck
One little flower, the flower forget-me-not,
And then afar beyond the clouds to fly
Higher and higher, and to disappear!
And thou didst hear me! Thou, with eagle pinions,
Monarch of birds, didst raise me to thyself.
O now, ye larks, I beg for nought from you,
For whither should she fly, what pleasures seek,

Who has the great God learned to know in heaven,
And loved a great man on this lower world?

KONRAD.

Greatness, and greatness yet again, mine angel!
Greatness for which we groan in misery!
A few days still,—let it torment the heart,—
A few days only, fewer already are.

[pg 26]

'Tis done! 'Tis vain to grieve for vanished time.
Aye! let us weep, but let our proud foes tremble!
For Konrad wept, but 'twas to murder them!
But wherefore cam'st thou here—wherefore, my love?
Unto God's service did I vow myself.
Was it not better in His holy walls,
Afar from me to live and die than here,
In the land of lying and of murderous war,
In this tower-grave by long and painful tortures
To expire, and open solitary eyes,
And through the unbroken fetters of this grate
Implore for help, and I be forced to hear,
To look upon the torture of long death,
Standing afar, and curse my very soul,
That harbours relics yet of tenderness?

VOICE FROM THE TOWER.

If thou lamentest, hither come no more!
Though thou shouldst come, with burning zeal implore,
Thou shouldst hear nought. My window now I close,
Descend once more into my prison darkness.

[pg 27]

Let me in silence drink my bitter tears.

Farewell for aye, farewell, my only one!

And let the memory perish of this hour,

Wherein thou didst no pity for me show.

KONRAD.

Then thou have pity! for thou art an angel!

Stay! But if prayer is powerless to restrain,

On the tower's angle will I strike my head;

I will implore thee by the death of Cain.

VOICE FROM THE TOWER.

O let us both have pity on ourselves!

My love, remember, great as is this world,

Two of us only on this mighty earth,

Upon the seas of sand two drops of dew.

Scarce breathes a little wind, from the earthly vale

For aye we vanish—ah! together perish!

I came not here for this, to torture thee.

I would not on me take the holy vows,

Because I dared not pledge my heart to Heaven,

While yet in it an earthly lover reigned.

I in the cloister would remain, and humbly

Devote my days to service of the nuns.

[pg 28]

But there without thee, everything around

Was all so new, so wild, so strange to me!

Remembering then that after many years,

Thou shouldst return again to Mary's town

To seek for vengeance on the enemy,

The cause defending of a hapless folk,

I said unto myself, "Who waits long years
Shortens with thoughts; maybe he now returns,
Maybe is come. Is it not free to ask,
Though living I immure me in the grave,
That once more I may look upon thyface,
That I at least may perish near to thee?
And therefore to the hermit's narrow house
Upon the road, upon the broken rock,
I will betake me, and enclose myself.
Some knight maybe, in passing by myhut,
May speak aloud by chance my loved one's name;
Among the foreign helmets I may view
His crest; though changed the fashion of his arms,
Although a strange device adorn his shield,
Although his face be changed, even then my heart
Will recognise my lover from afar.
And when a heavy duty him compels
To shed the blood of all and to destroy,
[pg 29]
And all shall curse him, one heart yet alone
Shall dare afar to bless him." Here I chose
My habitation and my grave apart,
In silence, where the sacrilege of groans
The traveller dare not listen. Thou, Iknow,
Lovest to walk alone. Within myself
I thought, "Maybe at even he will come,
Having his comrades left behind, to hold
Converse with winds and billows of the lake;
And he will think of me and hear myvoice."

And Heaven did fulfil my innocent wish.
Thou earnest; thou didst understand my song.
I prayed in former times that dreams might bless
Me with thine image, though the form were mute:
To-day, what happiness! To-day, together,—
Together we may weep!

KONRAD.

And wherefore weep?
I wept, thou dost remember, when I tore
Myself for ever from thy dear embrace,
And of my free will died fromhappiness,
That thus I might designs of blood fulfil.
That too long martyrdom at length is crowned.
[pg 30]
Now stand I at the summit of desires;
I can revenge me on the enemy.
And thou hast come to tear my victory from me!
Till now, when from the window of thy turret
Thou didst look on me, in the world's whole circle
Again there seemed no thing to meet my eye,
But the lake only, and the tower and grate.
Around me all with tumult seethes of war.
'Mid trumpet clamour, 'mid the clash of arms,
I seek impatient with a straining ear,
For the angelic sound of thy sweet lips,
And all the day for me is waiting hope.
And when the evening season I have reached,
I wish to lengthen it by memories:
I reckon by its evenings all my life.

Meanwhile the Order murmurs at repose,
Entreat for war, demand their own perdition;
And vengeful Halban will not let me breathe,
But still recalls to me those ancient vows,
The slaughtered hamlets, and the lands destroyed;
Or if I will not listen his reproaches,
He with one sigh, one glance, one beckoning,
Can blow my smouldering vengeance to a flame.
Now seems my destiny to near its end;
Nought the Crusaders can withhold from war.
[pg 31]
A messenger from Rome came yesterday.
From the world's every quarter, clouds unnumbered
A pious zeal hath gathered in the field,
And all call out to me to lead them on
With sword and cross upon the walls of Wilna.
And yet—with shame I must confess—ev'n now,
While destinies of mighty nations pend,
I think of thee, and still invent delays,
That we may pass together one more day.
O youth! how fearful was thy sacrifice!
When young, love, happiness, a veryheaven,
I for a nation's cause could sacrifice
With grief, but courage;—and to-day, grown old,—
To-day despair, my duty, and God's will
Compel me to the field, and still I dare not
Tear my grey head from these walls' pedestal,
That I may not forego thy sweet conversing.
He ceased. Groans only issued from thetower.

Long hours flowed by in silence. Now the night
Reddened, and now the water's stilly face
Blushed with the ray of dawn. Among the leaves
Of sleeping bushes with a rustling murmur
The morning freshness flew. The birds awoke
[pg 32]
With their soft notes, then once again they ceased,
And by long-during silence gave to know
They had too early woken. Konrad rose,
Lifted his eyes unto the tower, and looked
With anguish on the grate. The nightingale
Awoke in song, then Konrad looked around.
'Tis morning! and he let his visor down,
And in his cloak's wide folds concealed his face.
With beckoning of his hand he signs adieu,
And in the bushes how is lost

Ev'n thus,

A spirit infernal from a hermit's door
Doth vanish at the sound of matin bell.

[pg 33]

# IV.

# The festival.

It was the Patron's day, a solemn feast;
Komturs and brethren to the city ride;
White banners wave upon the castle towers:
Konrad invites the knights to festival.
A hundred white cloaks wave around the board,
On every mantle is the long black cross,—These
are the brethren, and behind them stand
The young esquires to serve them, in a ring.
Konrad sat at the top; upon his left
The place was Witold's,[8] with his leaders brave,—
One time their foe, to-day the Order's guest,
Leagued against Litwa as their firm ally.
The Master, rising, gives the festal word,
"Rejoice we in the Lord!" The goblets gleamed.
[pg 34]
"Rejoice we in the Lord!" cried thousand voices.
The silver shone, the wine poured forth in streams.
Silent sat Wallenrod, upon his elbow
Leaning, and heard with scorn the unseemly noise.

The uproar ceased; scarcely low-spoken jests
Alternate here and there the cup's lightclash.
"Let us rejoice," he says. "How now, my brethren!
Beseems it valiant knights to thus rejoice?
One time a drunken clamour, now low murmurs?
Must we then feast like bandits or like monks?
"There were far other customs in my time,
When on the battlefield with corpses piled,
On Castile's mountains or in Finland's woods,
We drank beside the camp-fire.
"Those were songs!
Is there no bard, no minstrel in the crowd?
Wine maketh glad indeed the heart of man,
But song it is that forms the spirit's wine."
[pg 35]
Then various singers all at once arose;
A fat Italian here, with birdlike tones,
Sings Konrad's valour and great piety;
And there a troubadour from the Garonne,
The stories of enamoured shepherds sings,
Of maids enchanted and of wandering knights.
Wallenrod slept;—meanwhile the songs are o'er.
Awakened sudden by the loss of sound,
He to the Italian cast a purse of gold.
"To me alone," he said, "thou didst sing praise.
Another may not give thee recompense;
Take and depart. Let that young troubadour,
Who serveth youth and beauty, pardon us
That in the knightly throng we have no damsel,

To fasten a vain rosebud to his breast

The roses here are faded. I wouldhave

Another bard,—the cloister knightdesires

Another song; but be it wild andharsh,

Like to the voice of horns, the clash of swords.

And be it gloomy as the cloister walls,

And fiery as a solitary drunkard.

"Of us, who sanctify and murder men,

Let song of murderous tone proclaim the saintship,

[pg 36]

And melt our heart, and rouse to rage,—and weary;

And let it then again affright the weary.

Such is our life, and such our song should be;

Who then will sing it?"

"I," replied an old

And venerable man, who near the door

Sat 'mid the squires and pages, by his robe

Prussian or Litwin. Thick his beard, by age

Whitened; the last grey hairs wave on his head;

His brow and eyes are covered by a veil;

Sufferings and years are graven on his face.

He bore in his right hand a Prussian lute,

But towards the table stretched his left hand forth,

And by this sign entreated audience.

All then were silent.

"I will sing," he cried.

"Once sang I to the Prussians and to Litwa;

Some now have perished in their land's defence;

Others will not outlive their country's loss,

But rather slay themselves upon her corse;
As servants true, in good and evil lot,
Will perish on their benefactor's pile.
[pg 37]
Others more shamefully in forests hide;
Others, like Witold, dwell among you here.
"But after death?—Germans! ye know full well.
Ask of the wicked traitors to their land
What, they shall do when, in that further world,
Condemned to burning of eternal fires,
They would their ancestors invoke from paradise?
What language shall entreat them for their aid?
If in their German, their barbaric speech,
The forefathers will know their children's voice.
"O children! what a foul disgrace for Litwa,
That none of you, aye, none, defended me,
When from the shrine, the hoary Wajdelote,[4]
Away they dragged me into German chains!
Alone in foreign lands have I grown old.
A singer!—alas! to no one can I sing!
On Litwa looking, I wept out mine eyes.
To-day, if I would sigh towards my home,
I know not where that home beloved lies,
If here, or there, or in another place.
"Here only, in my heart, have I preserved
That in my Fatherland my best possession;
[pg 38]
And these poor remnants of my former treasure
You Germans take from me,—take memory from me!

“As a defeated knight in tournament
Escapes with life though honour has been lost;
And, dragging out despisèd days in scorn,
Returns once more unto his conqueror;
And for the last time straining forth his arm,
Breaketh his sword beneath the victor’s feet,—
So my last failing courage me inspires;
Yet once more to the lute my hand is bold;
Let the last Wajdelote of Litwa sing
Litwa’s last song!”

He ended, and awaited
The Master’s answer. All in silence deep
Await. With mockery and with curious eye
Konrad tracks Witold’s every look and motion.
They noted all how when the Wajdelote
Of traitors spoke, a change o’er Witold came.
Livid he grew and pale again he blushed,
Alike tormented by his rage and shame.
At last, his sabre casting from his side,
He goes, dividing all the astonished crowd.
[pg 39]
He looked upon the old man, stayed his steps;
The clouds of anger hanging o’er his brow
Fell sudden in a rapid flood of tears;
He turned, sat down, with cloak he veiled his face,
And into secret meditation plunged
The Germans whispered, “Shall we to our feasts
Admit old beggars? Who will hear the song,
And who will understand?” Such voices were

Among the crowd of revellers, and broken
By constant peals of ever-growing laughter.
The pages cry, whistling on nuts, "Behold!
This is the tune of the Litvanian song."
Upon that Konrad rose. "Ye valiant knights!
To-day the Order, by a solemn custom,
Receiveth gifts from princes and from towns,
As homage from a conquered country due.
The beggar brings a song as offering
To you: forbid we not the old man's homage.
Take we the song; 'twill be the widow's mite.
"Among us we behold the Litwin prince;
His captains are the Order's guests: to him
Sweet will it be to list the memory
[pg 40]
Of ancient deeds, recalled in native speech.
Who understands not, let him go from hence.
I love betimes to hear the gloomy groans
Of those Litvanian songs, not understood,
Even as I love the noise of warring waves,
Or the soft murmur of the rain in spring;—
Sweetly they charm to sleep. Sing, ancient bard!"

Song of the Wajdelote.[9]

When over Litwa cometh plague and death,
The bard's prophetic eye beholds, afraid.
If to the Wajdelote's word be given faith,
On desert plains and churchyards, sayeth fame,
Stands visibly the pestilential maid,[10]
In white, upon her brow a wreath of flame,—

Her brow the trees of Bialowiez[11] outbraves,—
And in her hand a blood-stained cloth she waves.
The castle guards in terror veil their eyes,
The peasants' dogs, deep burrowing in the ground,
Scent death approaching, howl with fearful cries
The maid's ill-boding step, o'er all is found;
O'er hamlets, castles, and rich towns she goes.
[pg 41]
Oft as she waves the bloody cloth, no less
A palace changes to a wilderness;
Where treads her foot a recent grave up-grows.
O woeful sight! But yet a heavier doom
Foretold to Litwa from the German side,—
The shining helmet with the ostrich plume,
And the wide mantle with the black cross dyed.
For where that spectre's fearful step has passed,
Nought is a hamlet's ruin or a town,
But a whole country to the grave is cast
O thou to whom is Litwa's spirit dear!
Come, on the graves of nations sit we down;
We'll meditate, and sing, and shed the tear.
O native song! between the elder day,
Ark of the Covenant, and younger times,
Wherein their heroes' swords the people lay,
Their flowers of thought and web of native rhymes.
Thou ark! no stroke can break thee or subdue,
While thine own people hold thee not debased.
O native song! thou art as guardian placed,
[pg 42]

Defending memories of a nation's word.
The Archangel's wings are thine, his voice thine too,
And often wieldest thou Archangel's sword.
The flame devoureth story's pictured words,
And thieves with steel wide scatter treasure hoards.
But scatheless is the song the poet sings.
And should vile spirits still refuse to give
Sorrow and hope, whereby the song may live,
Upward she flieth and to ruins clings,
And thence relateth ancient histories.
The nightingale from burning dwellings flits,
But on the roof, a moment yet she sits;
When falls the roof she to the forest flies,
And from her laden breast o'er dying embers,
Sings a low dirge the passer-by remembers.
I heard the song! An ancient peasant swain,
When over bones his iron ploughshare rang,
Stood, and on flute of willow played a strain,
Prayers for the dead, or, with a rhymed lament,
Of you, great childless fathers, then he sang.
The echoes answered. I from far did hear,
[pg 43]
And sorrow brought the sight and song more near;
In eyes and ears my spirit all was bent.
As on the judgment-day the dead past all
The Archangel's trumpet from the tomb shall call,
So from the song the dead bones upward grew
To giant forms, from sleep of death awake,
Pillars and arches from their ruin anew,

And countless oars splashed in the desert lake;
And soon the castle-gates wide open seemed,
And princes' crowns and warriors' armour gleamed.
Now sing the bards, the dance the maidens weave;
I dreamed of marvels,—and awoke to grieve.
Forests and native hills are vanished,
And thought doth fail, on weary pinions fled,
And sinketh in a hidden stillness drear.
The lute is silent in my stiffened hand,
And 'mid the groan of comrades of my land,
The voices of the past I may not hear.
Still something of that youthful fire once mine
Smoulders within me, and at times its light
Wakens the soul and maketh memory bright.
Then memory, like a lamp of crystalline,
The pencil has with painted colours decked,
[pg 44]
Although by dust bedimmed, with scars beflecked;
Place but within its heart a little light,
With freshness of its colours eyes are lured,
On palace walls yet gleaming fair and bright,
Lovely, though yet with dusty cloud obscured.
O could I but this fire of mine impart
To all my hearers' breasts, the shapes upraise
Of those dead times, and reach the very heart
Of all my brothers with my burning lays!
But haply even in this passing hour,
Now when their native song their hearts can move,
The pulses of those hearts may beat more strong,

Their souls may feel the ancient pride and love;
And live one moment in such noble power,
As lived their forefathers their whole life long.
But why invoke the ages long gone by,
And for the present's glory find no voice?
For in your midst a great man liveth nigh—
I sing of him. Ye, Litwini, rejoice!
Silent the old man was, and hearkened round,
If still the Germans will permit his song.
Around the hall there reigned a silence deep;
[pg 45]
This warms all poets to a newer zeal.
Once more he raised his song, but other theme;
O'er freer cadences his voice did range.
More rarely he, and lighter, touched the strings,
Descending from the hymn to simple story.

THE WAJDELOTE'S TALE.

Whence come the Litwins? From a nightly sally;
From church and castle they have won rich spoils,
And crowds of German slaves with fettered hands,
Ropes on their necks, follow the victors' steeds.
They look towards Prussia and dissolve in tears,
On Kowno look, commend their souls to God.
In midst of Kowno stretches Perun's plain;
The Litwin princes, there returned from conquest,
Do burn the German knights in sacrifice.[12]
Two captive knights untroubled ride to Kowno,
One fair and young, the other bowed with years.
They in the battle left the German troops,

Fled to the Litwins. Kiejstut did receive them,
But led them to the castle under guard.
He asks their race, with what intent they come.
"I know not," said the youth, "my race or name;
In childhood was I made the Germans' captive.
[pg 46]
I recollect alone, somewhere in Litwa,
Amid a great town stood my father's house.
It was a wooden town on lofty hills,
The house was of red brick. Around the hills
Murmured a wood of fir-trees on the plains;
Among the woods a white lake gleamed afar.
One night a shout aroused us from our sleep;
A fiery day dawned in the window, shook
The window-panes, and whirling wreaths of smoke
Burst forth within the house. We to the door.
Flames curled through all the streets, sparks fell like hail.
A horrid cry arose, 'To arms! the Germans
Are in the town! to arms!' My father rushed
Forth with his sword,—rushed forth—returned no more!
The Germans poured into the house. One seized me
And caught me to his saddle. What came further
I know not; but long, long my mother's shrieks
I heard 'mid clash of swords, 'mid fall of houses.
This cry long followed me, stayed in my ear;
Even now when I view flames and falling houses,
This cry wakes in my soul as echo wakes
In caverns after thunder's voice. Behold
[pg 47]

My memories all of Litwa and my parents.
Sometimes in dreams I view the honoured forms
Of mother, father, brethren; but anew
Some cloud mysterious veils their features o'er,
Thicker and darker growing evermore.
The years of childhood passed away. I lived
A German among Germans, and they gave me
The name of Walter,[13] Alf thereto as surname.
German the name, my soul remained Litvanian;
Grief for my parents, for the strangers hatred
Remained. The Master Winrych in his palace
Reared me, himself did hold me to the font,
Loved and caressed me as his very son.
But weary in his palace, from his knees
I fled unto the Wajdelote. That time
Among the Germans was a Litwin bard,
Captive for many years,—interpreter,
He served the army. When he heard of me
That I was orphan and Litvanian,
He told of Litwa, cheered my longing soul
With his caresses, song, and with the sound
Of the Litvanian speech. He often led me
To the grey Niemen's shores; from thence I joyed
To look upon my country's well-loved mountains.
[pg 48]
And when unto the castle we returned,
He dried my tears to waken no suspicion:
He dried my tears, but kindled in me vengeance
Against the Germans. I remember well

How, when we came again into the castle,
I sharpened secretly a knife, with what
Delight of vengeance cut I Winrych's carpets,
Or broke his mirrors, on his shining shield
Flung sand, or spit upon it. Later on,
When grown near manhood, from Klajpedo's port
I sailed with the old man to view the shores
Of Litwa. There I plucked my country's flowers;
Their magic fragrance woke within my soul
Some ancient, dark remembrance. With the fragrance
Intoxicated, seemed me that a child
Once more I grew, and in my parents' garden,
Played with my little brothers. The old man
Assisted memory with his words, more lovely
Than herbs and flowers,—painted the happy past,
How sweet in native land 'mid friends and kin
To pass one's youth, how many Litwin children
Knew not such bliss, in the Order's fetters weeping.
I heard this on the plains, but on the beach,
Where the white billows break with roaring breasts,
[pg 49]
And from their foamy throat cast streams of sand,
'Thou seest,' the old man then was used to say,
'The grassy carpet of this seaboard meadow.
The sand blows over it. These fragrant herbs,
Thou seest, would pierce the deadly covering,
By their brow's strength. In vain, alas! for now
Another hydra comes of gravel-dust,
Spreads its white fins, subdues the living lands,

Stretching its kingdom of wild desert round.
My son! the gifts of spring are living cast
Into the grave. Behold! they are conquered peoples,
Our brothers the Litwini! Son, this sand
Storm-driven from the sea, it is the Order.'
My heart did pain me hearing, and I longed
To murder all Crusaders, or to fly
To Litwa; but the old man checked my zeal.
'To free knights,' said he, 'it is free to choose'
Their weapon, and with equal strength to fight
in open field. Thou art a slave; the only
Weapon that slaves may use is treachery.
Remain awhile and learn the Germans' war-craft;
Try thou to gain their confidence; we later
Shall see what thing to do.' I was obedient
Unto the old man's words—went with the Germans.
[pg 50]
But in the first fight, scarce I viewed the standards,
Scarce did I hear my, nation's songs of war,
I sprang unto our own,—led the old man with me.
As the young falcon, severed from his nest,
And nourished in a cage, although the fowlers
By cruel torments strip him of his reason,
And send him forth to war on brother-falcons;
Soon as he rises 'mid the clouds, soon as
His eyes o'erstretch the far unmeasured plains
Of his blue Fatherland, he breathes free air,
And hears the rustle of his wings.—Return
Unto thy home, O fowler! do not wait

To see the falcon in his narrow cage."

The youth made end; with wonder Kiejstut heard,

And listened also Kiejstut's daughter fair,

Aldona, young and lovely as a goddess.

The autumn passes, therewith evenings lengthen;

And Kiejstut's daughter, as accustomed, sits

Among her sisters and her comrades' train,

Weaves at the loom or spins the distaff thread;

But as the needles fly or spindles turn,

Walter stands by and telleth wondrous tales,

About the German countries and his youth.

The damsel seizes all that Walter speaks,

Her soul, insatiable, devours all things;

[pg 51]

She knows them all by heart, repeats in dreams.

Walter related of the castle halls,

Great towns beyond the Niemen, what rich dresses,

What splendid pastimes; how in tourney knights

Break lances, and the damsels look upon them

Down from their galleries, and adjudge the prize.

He spoke of the great God who rules beyond

The Niemen, and His Son's Immaculate Mother,

Whose angel form he showed in wondrous picture.

This picture piously adorned his breast;

The youth now gave it to the fair Litwinka,

The day he brought her to the holy faith,

When he prayed with her;—he would teach her all

He knew himself. Alas! he taught her too

That which as yet he knew not,—taught her love.

And he himself learned much. With what delight
He from her lips the half-forgotten words
Heard of Litvanian speech. New feelings rose
With each new-risen word like sparks from ashes.
Sweet were the names of family, of friendship,
And sweeter yet than all the name of love,
Which no word equals here on earth, but—country.
"Whence," Kiejstut thought, "my daughters sudden change?
[pg 52]
Where is her former mirth, her childish sports?
On holidays all maidens join in dance;
She sits alone, or converse holds with Walter.
On other days the needle or the loom
Engage the damsels; from her hands the needle
Falls, and the threads are tangled in the loom.
She sees not what she does; all tell me so.
And yesterday, I marked she sewed a rose,
The flowers with green, the leaves with rosy silk.
How could she know this, when her eyes and thoughts
Seek only Walter's eyes, seek his discourse?
Oft as I ask, 'Where goes she?' 'To the valley.'
'Whence comes she?' 'From the valley.' 'What is there?'
'The youth has made in it a garden for her.'
What! is that garden fairer than my orchards?
(For Kiejstut owned proud orchards full of apples
And pears, allurement of the Kowno damsels.)
'Tis not the garden lures her. I have marked
Her windows in the winter; all the panes
Which look on Niemen clear are as in May;

The frost has not obscured the crystal glass.
Thence Walter comes. She sat beside the window,
And with her burning sighs did melt the ice.
[pg 53]
I thought, he teaches her to read and write,
Hearing all princes now instruct their children,—
A good lad, valiant, skilled like priest in books.
Shall I expel him from my house? He is
So needful to our Litwa; he can rank
The troops as can no other; rampart mounds
He best can heap; the thunder-arms direct.
I have one behind my army.—Walter, come,
And be my son-in-law, and fight for Litwa."
So Walter wed Aldona. Germans! you
No doubt will think this is the story's end;
For in your love romances when the knights
Are married, then the minstrel ends his song,
And only adds, "They lived long and were happy."
Well Walter loved his wife; his noble soul
Yet found no happiness in heart or home,
For in the country was there blessing none.
The snows scarce vanished, scarce the first lark sung;—
The lark to other lands sings love and joy,
But unto hapless Litwa he proclaims
With every year carnage and fire;—on march
Crusading armies in unnumbered crowds.
Now from the hills beyond the Niemen echo
[pg 54]
To Kowno bears a mighty army's shouts,

The clang of armour and the neigh of steeds.
Like mist the camp descends, o'erflows the plain,
And here and there the leaders' standards gleam
Like lightning ere the storm. The Germans stood
Upon the shore, threw bridges o'er the Niemen,
And day by day the walls and bastions fall
With shock of battering-ram, and night by night
The storming mines work underground like moles;
Beneath the heavens the bomb in fiery flight
Rises, and swoops upon the city roofs,
As falls the falcon on the lesser fowl.
Kowno is fallen in ruins. Then the Litwin
Retires to Kiejdan; Kiejdan falls in ruin.
Then Litwa makes defence in woods and hills;
The Germans march on farther, robbing, burning;
Kiejstut and Walter first in battle, last
Retreating. Kiejstut was untroubled still,
From childhood used to combat with his foe,
To attack, to conquer, or to fly. He knew
His forefathers warred ever with the Germans;
He, following in their footsteps, ever fought,
And cared not for the future. Other were
The thoughts of Walter. Nurtured 'mid theGermans,
[pg 55]
He knew the Order's power; the Master's summons,
He knew, could draw forth armies, treasures, swords,
From all of Europe. Prussia made defence;
In former times the Teutons broke thePrussians;
Sooner or later Litwa meets such fate.

He had seen the Prussians' misery; he trembled
To think of Litwa's future. "Son," cries Kiejstut,
"Thou art an evil prophet; thou hast reft
The veil before my eyes, to show the abyss.
While hearing thee, it seemed my hands grew weak,
With victory's hope all courage left my breast
How shall we with the German power contend?"
"Father," said Walter, "one sole way I know,
A dreadful way, alas! effectual!
Some day I may reveal it." Thus did they
Converse, the battle over, ere the trumpet
Did summon to fresh battles and defeats.
Kiejstut grew ever sadder, and how changed
Seemed Walter; never over-merry he.
Even in happy moments some light shade
Of thought o'erhung his brow, but with Aldona
Serene was once his brow and visage tranquil,
Aye welcoming her with smiles, with tender glance
Bidding farewell to her. Now, as it seemed,
He was tormented by some hidden pain.
[pg 56]
By morn, before the house, wringing his hands,
He looked upon the smoke of towns and hamlets,
Burning far off; there gazed he with wildeyes.
By night he started out of sleep, and looked
Forth from the window on the blood-red blaze.
"Husband, what ails thee?" asks with tears Aldona.
"What ails me? Shall I peaceful sleep till Germans
Shall give me sleeping, bound, tohangman's hands?"

"O husband! Heaven forbid! The sentries guard
Full well the trenches." "True the sentries guard them.
I watch and grasp the sabre in my hand.
But when the sentries die the sword is broken.
List, if I live to old age, wretched age——"
"But Heaven will give us comfort in our children."
"The Germans will fall on us, slay the wife,
The children tear away, and lead them far,
Teach them to loose the arrow on their father.
Myself my father, brothers, might have slain,
Unless the Wajdelote——" "Dear Walter! go we
Farther in Litwa; hide we from the Germans
In mountains and in forests." "Aye, we go,
And other mothers, children leave behind.
Thus fled the Prussians; Germans overtook them
[pg 57]
In Litwa. If they trace us in the mountains——"
"Let us again go farther." "Farther? farther?
Unhappy one! shall we go far from Litwa,
Into the Tartar's or the Rusin's hands?"
Hushed was Aldona, troubled at this answer,
For hitherto it had to her appeared
Her Fatherland were long as is the world,
Wide without end; and now for the first time
She heard there was no refuge in all Litwa.
Wringing her hands she asked, "What may be done?"
"One way, Aldona, one remains to Litwa
To break the Order's power: that way I know;
But ask it not for God's sake. Hundred times

Be cursed that hour in which, constrained by foes,
I seize these means." No farther would he say,
Heard not Aldona's prayers, but only heard
And saw before him Litwa's misery.
At last the flame of vengeance, nursed in silence,
By sight of suffering and defeat, increased,
And did surround his heart, consumed all feelings—
One feeling even, hitherto life-sweetening,—
Feeling of love. So when the hunters light
A hidden fire 'neath oaks of Bialowiez,
It burns away the inner pith; the monarch
[pg 58]
Of the forest loses all his waving leaves,
His branches fly off, even that green crown
That once adorned his brow, the mistletoe,
Dries up and withers.
Long the Litwini
Wandered through castles, mountains, and through woods,
The Germans harrying or by them attacked,
Till fought the dreadful fight on Rudaw's plains,
Where many thousand Litwin youth lay slaughtered,
Beside as many of the Teuton host
Soon reinforcements from beyond the sea
Came to the Germans. Kiejstut then and Walter
Ascended with a handful to the mountains.
With broken sabres and with dinted shields,
Covered with dust and clotted gore, they went
Gloomy towards home. There Walter neither looked
Upon his wife, nor spoke to her one word;

But in the German tongue held he discourse
With Kiejstut and the Wajdelote. Aldona
Nought understood, but yet her heart forebode
Some dire event When ended was their council,
All three turned sorrowing glances on Aldona.
Walter looked longest, with despair's mute gaze;
[pg 59]
Thick-falling teardrops trickled from his eyes;
He fell before Aldona's feet and pressed
Her hands unto his heart, and pardon begged
For all the things that she had suffered of him.
"Woe!" cried he, "unto women loving madmen,
Whose hearts domestic happiness contents not.
Great hearts, Aldona, are like hives too large;
Honey can fill them not, and they become
The lizard's nest. Forgive me, dear Aldona!
To-day I would remain at home, to-day
Forget all things; be we for each to-day
What once we used to be. To-morrow——" But
He could not finish. What joy then Aldona's!
She thought, unhappy, Walter would be changed,
That he would live in peace and joyousness.
Less thoughtful did she see him, in his eyes
More life; she saw new colour in his cheeks;
And all that evening at Aldona's feet
Spent Walter. Litwa, Teutons, and the war
He cast awhile into forgetfulness;
Talked of those happy times when first he came
To Litwa, his first converse with Aldona,

The first walk to the valley, and of all
Those childish things, but memorable to the heart,
Of that first love. Wherefore such sweet discourse
[pg 60]
Must he break off with that sad word—to-morrow,
And plunge in thought, look long upon his wife?
Tears circle in his eyes. Would he then speak,
But dares not? Did he but invoke the feelings,
The memories of ancient happiness,
Only to bid farewell to them? Shall all
This evening's converse, all its sweet caresses,
Be but the last, last flickerings of love's torch?
'Tis vain to ask. Aldona looks and waits,
Uncertain. Passing from the room, she gazed
Still through the crannies. Walter poured out wine,
And emptied many cups, and near him kept
The hoary Wajdelote through all the night.
Scarce risen had the sun when hoofs were clattering;
Up with the morning mists two riders haste;
The guards all missed them; one eye could not miss.
A lover's eyes are vigilant. Aldona
Had guessed their flight; she rushed into the valley.
Sad was that meeting. "O my love, return!
Return thou home—return! Thou must be happy,
Blest in embraces of thy family.
Thou art young and fair; comfort will soon be thine.
Forget me. Many princes formerly
[pg 61]
Contended for thy hand. And thou art free,

Being as widow left of a great man,
Who for his country's weal renounced ev'n thee!
Farewell! forget; but weep for me at times;
For Walter loses all; he doth remain
Lone as the lone wind in thewilderness,
And he must wander over all the world,
To plunder, murder, and at last to perish
By shameful death. But after vanished years
The name of Alf again shall sound in Litwa,
And from the Wajdelote's lips thou shalt again
Hear of his deeds. Then, loved one, think thou then,
This dreadful knight, with cloud of mystery veiled,
Is known to thee alone,—was once thy husband;
And be thy pride thy desolation's comfort."
Silent Aldona did assent, although
She heard no word. "Thou goest! thou goest!" she cried,
And her own anguish wrought with her own words.
"Thou goest!" this one word sounded in her ear.
She framed no thought, nothing recalled; her thoughts,
Her memories, her future, tangled all;
But guessed her heart she never could return,
[pg 62]
Nor e'er forget. Her eyes all wandering roved,
And many times met Walter's wildered look,
Wherein she might not find the ancient joy;
She seemed to seek for something new around,
And looked once more. 'Twas forestwilderness.
Beyond the Niemen 'mid the forests gleamed
A turret height; a convent 'twas of nuns,

Sad dwelling of the Christians. On this tower
Rested Aldona's eyes and thoughts; the dove
Seized by the wind amidst a raging sea,
Thus falls upon an unknown vessel's mast.
And Walter understood Aldona. Silent
He followed her, and told her his design,
Commanding secrecy before the world.
And at the doors—ah! fearful was that parting!
Alf rode off with the Wajdelote. Till now
Nought has been heard of them. But woe to him
If he fulfil not hitherto his vows,
If, having all his bliss renounced and poisoned
Aldona's happiness, and sacrificed
So much, he still have sacrificed in vain!
The future shows the rest. I have ended, Germans.
This is the end?—great murmur in the hall.
"Who is this Walter, and what are his deeds?
[pg 63]
Where? vengeance upon whom?" the hearers cried.
The Master only, 'mid the murmuring crowd,
In silence sat with head bent down. He seemed
As deeply moved; each instant snatches cups
Of wine, and to the very bottom drains.
Upon him came a change of somewhat new,
Many emotions break in sudden lightnings,
And circle o'er his burning countenance;
His pale lips quiver, and his wandering eyes
Fly round like swallows in the midst of storm.
At last he cast his mantle off, and sprang

Into the midst. "Where is the story's end?
Sing me at once the end or give the lute.
Why stand'st thou trembling? Give the lute to me.
Fill up the goblets; I will sing the end
If thou dost fear to sing it.
"I know ye. Every song the Wajdelote sings
Portendeth woe, as howls of dogs at night.
Murders and burnings ye delight to sing,
Ye leave to us—glory and sorrowing.
Yet in the cradle doth your traitorous song
Circle the infant's breast in reptile form,
And cruellest poison sheds into the soul,
Foolish desire of praise and patriot love.
[pg 64]
"She follows hard the footsteps of a youth
Like shade of slaughtered foe, sometimes reveals
Herself in midst of banquets, mixing blood
In cups of joy. I have heard the song—too well,
Alas! Tis done, 'tis done! I know thee, traitor!
Thou winnest! War! what triumph for a poet!
Give to me wine; now my designs are working.
"I know the song's end. No! I'll sing another.
When on the mountains of Castile I fought,
There the Moors taught me ballads. Old man! play
That melody, that childish melody,
Which in the valley,—'twas a blessed time;
Unto that music did I ever sing.
Return at once, old man, for by all gods,
German or Prussian——"

The old man must return.

He struck the lute, and with uncertain voice
Followed the savage tones of Konrad, as
A slave may walk behind his angry lord.
Meanwhile the lights went out upon the table.
The knights had slumbered at the lengthy banquet,
But Konrad sings, and they awake again.
They stand, and, in a narrow circle pressed,
Attentive marked the ballad's every word.

[pg 65]

## BALLAD.

### ALPUJARA.

Ruined lie the Moorish cities,
Still the Moors upraise the sword;
In the country still resisting,
Reigns the pestilence as lord.
And the towers of Alpujara
Brave Almanzor still defends:
Floats below the Spaniard's banner,
Siege to-morrow he intends.
Roar the guns at sunrise loudly,
Ramparts break, and crumblewalls;
From the towers the cross gleamsproudly,—
Now the Spaniard owns these halls.
Sad Almanzor views his warriors
Slain in battle desperate;
Hews his way through swords andlances,
Flieth Spain's pursuing hate.
Now the Spaniards in the fortress,

'Mid the stones and corpses there,
Hold the feast and drain thewine-cup,
And the spoils and captives share.
[pg 66]
Soon the guard.without announces
That a stranger knight doth wait,
Craving for a swift admittance,
Bringing tidings of great weight
'Twas the vanquished Moor Almanzor.
Swift his mantle off was thrown;
To the Spaniards he surrenders,
And he craves for life alone.
"I am come, ye Christian warriors,
To submit me to your power;
I will serve the God of Christians,
Own your prophet from this hour,
"Let the blast of fame, world-filling,
Say, the Arab chief o'erthrown
Would be brother to his victors,
Vassal of a stranger's crown."
Well the Spaniard prizes valour.
So the great Almanzor knowing,
They embraced him, circled roundhim,
As their true companionshowing.
Each one then Almanzor greeted,
And their captain closeembraced:
[pg 67]
Hung upon his neck, and kissed him;
Such true love their friendship graced.

All at once his strength grew feebler,
  And he fell upon the ground;
But he drew the Spaniard with him,
  To his feet the turban bound.
All with wonder looked upon him,
  And his livid visage scan;
Horrid smiles deformed his features,
  And with blood his eyes o'erran.
"Christian dogs," he cries, "look on me,
  If you understand this thing;
I deceived you, from Granada
  Come I, and the plague I bring.
"For my kiss breathed venom in ye,
  And the plague shall lay you low;
Come and look upon my tortures—
  Ye such death must undergo."
Wide he cast his eyes around him,
  As he would eternally
Chain all Spaniards to his bosom;
  And a horrid laugh laughed he.

[pg 68]

Laughed, and died; his eyes yet open,
  Open yet his lips remained:
In that hellish smile for ever
  Those cold features still were strained.
Fled the Spaniards from the city.
  But the plague their steps pursuing,
Ere they left doomed Alpujara,
  Was that gallant host's undoing.

"Thus years ago the Moors avenged themselves;
Would you the vengeance of the Litwin know?
What if some day it issue forth in words,
And come to mingle poison in the wine?
But no! ah, no! to-day are other customs,
Prince Witold; for to-day the Litwin lords
Come to deliver us their native land,
And seek for vengeance on their harassed people.
"But yet, indeed, not all—oh! no, by Perun!
There are in Litwa yet—I'll sing yet to you!
Away from me that lute—a string is broken.
No song will be—but I do trust indeed
One time there will be. This day, o'er filled cups,—
[pg 69]
I have drunk too much—rejoice yourselves and play!
And thou Al—manzor, leave my sight, old man!
Away with Halban—leave me here alone."
He said, and turning by uncertain way,
He found his place, and sank into his chair.
Still threatening somewhat, stamping with his foot,
O'erturned the table with the wine and cups.
At last grown weaker, he inclined his head
Upon the chair-arm; soon his glance was quenched;
His quivering lips were covered o'er with foam.
He slept.
The knights awhile in fixed amazement stood:
They knew full well Konrad's unhappy custom;
How, when inflamed unto excess with wine,
Into wild transports and forgetfulness

He falls; but at a banquet, public shame!

Before the strangers, in such unheard rage!

Who thus inflamed him? Where that Wajdelote?

He vanished privately, none know of him.

Stories there were that Halban thus disguised

To Konrad that Litvanian song had sung,

[pg 70]

To kindle by this means the zeal of Christians

To battle against heathenesse; but whence

A change so sudden in the Master? Wherefore

Did Witold show such angry wrath? Whatmeans

The Master's strange, wild ballad? With conjectures,

Each vainly tries to track the hidden secret.

---

[pg 71]

# V.

## War.[14]

War now. For Konrad may no longer curb
The people's zeal, the council's fierce insistance:
The whole land calls for vengeance long delayed,
For Litwa's inroad, and for Witold's treason.
Witold, once suitor for the Order's grace,
To aid recovery of his capital,
After the banquet, on this new report
That the Crusading hosts will take the field,
Changed measures—traitor to his recent friendship,
And led his knights in secrecy away.
And in the Teuton castles on the road
He entered, by the Master's forged commands;
And then disarming all the garrison,
Annihilated all with fire and sword.
The Order, roused with burning rage and shame,
Against the heathens stirred up fierce Crusade;
The Pope sends forth a bull,—seas, land, o'erflow
[pg 72]
At once with swarms of warriors numberless,

Princes with mighty following of vassals;
The Red Cross decks their armour. Each his life
Devotes to christen pagans,—or to die.
They went towards Litwa. What their actions there?
If thou wouldst know, gaze from the ramparts' heights,
Look towards Litwa, as the day declines.
Thou see'st a fiery blaze; the vault of heaven
O'er-deluged with a stream of bloody flame;
Behold the annals of invading war.
Few words relate their carnage, plunder, fire,
And blaze, which may rejoice the foolish crowd,
But in it wise men do with fear confess,
A voice that crieth for revenge to Heaven.
The winds blew on that dreadful fire apace,
The knights marched further to the heart of Litwa.
Report says Kowno, Wilna, are besieged.
Then ceased report, and couriers came no more.
No longer in the region flames were seen,
But further off the heaven's ruddy blaze.
In vain the Prussians look with eager hope,
[pg 73]
For spoils and prisoners of the conquered land;
In vain despatch swift couriers for the news,
The couriers hasten—and return no more.
As each this cruel doubt interpreteth,
He willingly would know despair itself.
The autumn passed away. The winter's snows
Revelled upon the mountains, block the ways.
Once more upon the distant heaven shine—

Midnight auroras? or the fires of war?
And ever nearer comes the light of flames,
And nearer yet the heaven's ruddy blaze.
From Marienbourg the folk look on the road;
They see afar—grovelling through deepest snows,
Some travellers!—Konrad! And our generals!
How welcome them? Victors? or fugitive?
Where are the others? Konrad raised his hand,
And pointed further off a scattered crowd,
Alas! their very aspect told the secret!
They rush in disarray, plunge in the snowdrifts;
Roll each on each, down treading like vile insects,
Within a narrow vessel perishing;
They push o'er corpses, ever newer crowds,
Hurl those new risen down again to earth.
[pg 74]
Some drag still onward chilled and stiffened limbs,
Some on the march have frozen to the road;
But with raised hands the corpses standing point
Straight to the town, like pillars on the way.
The townsfolk, terror-stricken, curious ran,
Fearing to guess the truth they dared not ask;
For all the story of that luckless war
They in the warriors' eyes and faces read
For o'er their eyes hung death in frosty shape,
And Famine's harpy hollowed out their cheeks.
Now are the trumpets of the Litwin heard,
Now rolls the storm, snow whirlwinds o'er the plain;
Far off a multitude of gaunt dogs howls,

And overhead the ravens hover round.
All perished! Konrad has destroyed them all!
He, that once reaped such glory with the sword,
He, for his prudence formerly renowned,
Timid and careless in this latter war,
Marked not the cunning snares that Witold laid;
Deceived and blinded by the wish of vengeance,
Driving his army on the Litwin steppes,
Wilna thus long in sluggard guise besieged.
[pg 75]
When plunder and provisions were consumed,
When hunger came upon the German camp,
And scattered all around, the enemy
Destroyed the auxiliars, cut off all supplies,
Each day a myriad Germans died from need.
Now time approached to end by storm the war,
Or else bethink them of a swift return.
Then Wallenrod, in peace and confidence,
Rode to the chase, or, closed within his tent,
Forged secret treaties, and denied his captains
Admission to the councils of the war.
And thus in warlike fervour grew he cold,
That by his people's tears untouched, unmoved,
He deigned not raise the sword in their defence;
All day with folded arms upon his breast,
In thought remaining, or discourse with Halban.
Meanwhile the winter piled its heaps of snow,
And Witold, with his fresh recruited bands,
Besieged the army, fell upon the camp.

Oh! shame in annals of the valiant Order!
The Master first did fly the battle-field!
In place of laurels, and abundant spoil,
He brought the news of Litwa's victories!
[pg 76]
Did ye but mark, when from that thunder stroke
He led this host of spectres to their homes,
What gloomy sadness darkened o'er his brow?
The worm of pain unwound him from his cheek,
And Konrad suffered; but look on his eyes!
That large half-open eye, bright shining throws
Its darts aslant, like comet threatening war;
Each moment changing, like the gleams of night,
Whereby the wily demon travellers lures.
Uniting joy and rabid rage in one,
It shone as with a right Satanic glance.
Trembled the folk and murmured. Konrad care not.
He called to council the unwilling knights,
Looked on them, spoke, and beckoned. O disgrace!
They hear attentive, and believe his words.
They view Heaven's judgments in the faults of man;
For whom of humankind persuades not—anguish.
Tarry, proud ruler! Judgment waits even thee!
In Malborg is a dungeon underground.
There, when the night in darkness wraps the town,
The secret tribunal descends to council.15
[pg 77]
One single lamp upon the high-arched roof,
And day and night it burns mysteriously.

Twelve chairs, in circle placed around a throne,—
Upon the throne the secret book of laws.
Twelve judges each in sable armour clad;
The visages of all inlocked by masks,
In dungeons hide them from the common crowd;
But each thus masked enshrouds him from his fellows.
All sworn, of their own will, with one accord,
Crimes of their potent rulers to chastise,
Too heinous, or unknown before the world.
And soon as falls on him the last decree,
Not even a brother's trespass to condone;
Each must by violent or by treasonous ways,
On him condemned fulfil the spoken doom;
Dagger in hand, and rapier at their side.
One of the maskers now approached the throne,
And standing with drawn sword before the book,
Spoke thus: "Tremendous judges!
Proof now our long suspicion hasconfirmed.
That man who calls him Konrad Wallenrod,
He is not Wallenrod.
[pg 78]
Who is he? 'Tis unknown. Twelve years ago,
From unknown parts he to the Rhine-land came.
When passed Count Wallenrod to Palestine,
He in the count's train wore an esquire's dress.
But soon Count Wallenrod, unknown, didperish.
And then his squire, suspected of his death,
Departed secretly fromPalestine;
Then did he land upon the Spanish shore;

In battles with the Moors gave proof of valour,
And in the tourneys prizes rich obtained,
And everywhere gained fame as Wallenrod.
He took on him at length the Order's vows,
Was chosen Master, to the Order's loss.
How ruled he, all ye know. This latter winter
When we with frost, famine, and Litwa fought,
Konrad in woods and oak-groves rode alone;
And there in secret held discourse with Witold.
Long time my spies have traced his every deed;
Hidden at evening by the corner tower,
They understood not the discourse which Konrad
Did hold with the recluse;—but, dreadful judges,
He spoke, they said, in the Litvanian tongue.
And weighing duly what the messengers
Of our tribunal of this man reported,
And that intelligence my spy late brought,
[pg 79]
And fame reporteth, scarcely secretly;
Tremendous judges! I accuse the Master
Of falsehood, murder, heresy, and treason."
Here the accuser knelt before the book,
And laid his hand upon the crucifix;
And with an oath confirmed his story's truth,
By God, and by the Saviour's agony.
He ceased. The judges arbitrate the cause,
But not by open voice or still discourse;
Scarce by a glance of eye, or sign of hand,
Their deep and dreadful thought communicate.

Each in his turn approached him to the throne,
And with the dagger's point o'erturned the leaves,
Of the Order's book, and silent read the law,
Inquiring sentence of his conscience only.
And having judged, his hand lays on his heart,
And all in concord raised the cry of "Woe!"
With threefold echo then the walls repeated,
"Woe!"—In that word alone, that single word,
A sentence lies! The arraigners understood.
Twelve swords were raised aloft; one aim was theirs—
Destined to Konrad's heart. Then all departed
In gloomy silence, and the walls behind,
Repeated with a fearful echo: "Woe!"
[pg 80]

# VI

# The Parting.

A WINTRY dawn, with stormy wind and snow;
Through storm and snow-clouds hastens Wallenrod.
Scarce stands he on the borders of the lake,
He calls aloud, striking the tower with sword.
"Aldona," cries he, "let us live, Aldona!
Thy lover comes; his vows are all fulfilled,
The foes have perished, all is now fulfilled."

THE RECLUSE.

"Alf! 'tis his voice indeed! My Alf, my love!
What! peace already! thou returnest safe?
Thou goest not forth again?"

KONRAD.

"For love of God,
Ask thou no tidings!—Listen, my beloved!
Listen, and weigh with carefulness each word,
[pg 81]
The foes have perished. Dost thou see these fires?
Thou see'st? 'Tis Litwa's havoc with the Germans.
A hundred years heal not the Order's wounds,
I smote the hundred-headed monster's heart.
Their treasures wasted, well-springs of their power,
Their towns in flames, a sea of blood has flowed,—
I caused all this! I have fulfilled my vows!
More fearful vengeance hell might not conceive.
I will no more of it—I am a man!
I spent my youth in foul hypocrisy,
In bloody, murders. Now, bent down with age,
Wearied of treasons, I am unfit for war.
Enough of vengeance. Germans, too, are men!
God has enlightened me. I come from Litwa,
And I have seen those places, seen thy castle,
The Kowno castle,—now it lies in ruin.
I turned away, urged thence my rapid course;
And hurried to that valley, our own valley.
All was as formerly! Those woods, those flowers!
All as it was upon that very eve,

When to the valley breathed we long farewell.

Alas! it seems to me but yesterday!

That stone—rememberest thou that high-raised stone

Once of our rambles limit made and end?

[pg 82]

It standeth now, though overgrown with moss;

Scarce might I view it, hidden thus in green.

I tore the herb off, watered it with tears.

That grassy seat, where, through the summer noon,

Thou didst among the maples love to rest;

That spring, whose waters then I sought for thee—

I found them all, looked on them, passed around.

And even thy little arbour still remains,

As with dry willow-twigs I fenced it in;

And those dry twigs, a wonder, my Aldona,

That once I planted in the barren sand,

To-day thou wouldst not know them—lovely trees,

And the light leaves of spring upon them wave,

And on them grows the youthful catkin's down.

Oh! seeing these, a blessing all unknown,

Foreshadowing of joy, revived my heart;

The trees embracing, on my knees I fell

O God! I cried, grant all may be fulfilled!

Oh! may we, to our Fatherland restored,

When dwelling in our Litwa's native fields,

Again revive to life; may leaves of hope

Again o'erdeck with green our destiny.

Let us return! consent! I rule the Order;

I will bid open. But what need commands?

For were this door a thousand times more hard

[pg 83]

Than steel, I'd beat it down—I'd pluck it up;

And thee, O my beloved, to our valley,

There will I lead thee, raise thee with my hand.

Or go we further still? Litwa has deserts;

There lie deep shades in woods of Bialowiez,

Where never rings the clang of foreign swords,

Nor sounds the haughty victor's signal-word—

No, nor the groanings of our vanquished brothers.

There, in the midst of silent, pastoral joy,

And in thine arms, and on thy bosom, let me

Forget that there are nations in the world;

Or any worlds; we for ourselves will live—

Return, oh! speak, consent!"

Aldona spoke not;

And Konrad, silent, waited yet reply:

Meanwhile the blood-red dawn shone forth in heaven.

"O God! Aldona, morning is before us,

And men will wake: the guard arrest us here.

Aldona!"—called he, trembling withdespair.

No voice was his; beseeching with his eyes,

He lifted to the tower his claspèd hands,

Fell on his knees, and pity to entreat,

Embraced and kissed the walls of that cold tower.

[pg 84]

The Recluse.

"No, no! the time is past," her sad voice spoke;

"But be thou tranquil, Heaven will give me strength,

The Lord will shield me from that heaviest stroke.
When here I came, I on the threshold swore
Never to leave this tower, but for the grave.
I wrestled with myself, and thou, my love,
Thou, even thou, against the Lord wouldst aid me.
Wouldst give back to the world a wretched phantom?
Oh think! oh think! if madly I should give
Myself to be persuaded, leave this cave
And fall with rapture into thine embrace;
But thou wouldst know not, neither welcome me,
Avert thine eyes, and ask, with horror struck,
'What, is this fearful spectre fair Aldona?'
And thou wouldst seek in this extinguished eye,
And in this visage her—the thought is death!
No, never let the poor recluse's woe
Offend the beauty of the bright Aldona!
"Myself, I will confess, forgive me, love!
Oft as the moon with brighter lustre gleams,
Hearing thy voice, I hide behind these walls,
[pg 85]
Unwishing, loved one, to behold thee near!
For thou, maybe, art not the same to-day
Which once thou wert, in those sweet years gone by,
When with our hosts didst to our castle ride.
But thou retainest, hidden in my breast,
Those self-same eyes, that posture, form, and dress.
So the fair moth, within the amber drowned,
Retains its primal form eternally.
O Alf! 'twere better far that we remain

That which we were in former days, and as
We shall unite again,—but not on earth.
“Leave we the beauteous valleys to the happy,
I love the stony stillness of my cell;
For me ’tis bliss enough to see thee living,
And in the evening thy loved voice to hear.
And in this silence, Alf, beloved, we may
Heal every suffering, sweeten every pang,
All treasons, murders, burnings, cast aside,
Strive thou to come but earlier and more frequent.
“If thou shouldst—listen, on these very plains,
Like to that arbour plant another bower,
And hither bring those willows that thou lovest,
[pg 86]
And flowers, and even that stone from out the valley;
There let the children from the hamlet near,
Play joyously beneath their native trees,
And into garlands weave their native plants;
Let them repeat the Lithuanian songs,
For native song doth meditation aid,
And brings me dreams of Litwa and of thee.
And later, later, when my life is o’er,
Here let them sing, and on the grave of Alf.”
Alf heard no longer; he, on that wild shore,
Wandered on aimless, without thought or will;
A mountain there of ice, a forest there
Allured him; savage sights and hasty course
Afforded him relief in weariness.
His breast was heavy in the winter rain,

He cast aside his mantle, coat-of-mail,
He tore his garments, from his breast threw off
All—all but sorrow!
Now morning lighted on the city ramparts.
He saw an unknown shadow, stopped, and gazed—
The shadow further moved; with silent steps
It glided o'er the snow, and disappeared
[pg 87]
Within the trenches, but a voice was heard
Three times that voice repeated: "Woe, woe, woe!"
Alf at this voice awoke, and stood in thought
He thought awhile,—and understood the whole.
He drew his sword, and looked to every side;
He turned him round, searched with unquiet eye—
'Twas waste around; only the winter snow
Flew in a whirlwind, and the north wind roared
He looked upon the shore, he stood in grief.
At length with rapid stride, though tottering,
He came again beneath Aldona's tower.
Far off he saw her, at the window still.
"Good day!" he cried; "so many, many years,
We saw each other only in the night.
And now good day! what happy augury!
The first good day after so many years!
And canst thou guess, wherefore I come so soon?"

ALDONA.

"I will not guess. Farewell, belovèd friend!
The light has risen too brightly—if they knew thee—
[pg 88]

Cease to importune me. Farewell till evening.
I cannot come forth—will not"

ALF.

"Tis too late.
Know'st thou for what I pray thee? Throw some twig;
No, no, thou hast no flowers. From thy garments
A thread, or from thy tresses cast a lock;
Or throw a pebble from thy prison walls.
To-day I wish—all may not see to-morrow.
I would to-day have some remembrance of thee,
That lay this very morn upon thy breast,
And which a tear shall glow on, lately shed,
For I would lay it on my heart in death,
And bid the gift farewell with my last breath.
I must die shortly, swiftly, suddenly!
Well die together! Dost thou see thatshot-hole?
There will I dwell. Each morning for a sign,
I'll hang a black cloth on the balcony,
And at the grate each evening place a lamp.
There gaze thou steadfast. Throw I down the cloth,
Or if the lamp expires before its time,
Close thou thy window. I maybe return not.
Farewell, beloved!"

[pg 89]

He vanished. Still Aldona
Gazed, bending downward from the window grate.
The morn had passed away, the sun had set,
But her white garments, dallying in the wind,
And arms stretched down to earth were long beheld.

“The sun has set at last,” spoke Alf to Halban,
And pointed from his shot-hole to the sun.
Within the turret, from the early morn
He sat, and looked upon Aldona’s window,
“Give me my cloak and sword. Farewell, true friend;
I go unto the tower. Farewell for long,
Maybe for ever!—Listen to me, Halban.
If, when to-morrow day begins to gleam,
I come not back, leave thou this dwelling-place.
I will, I would give something to thy charge.
How lone am I! either in earth or heaven,
To no one, nowhere, have I aught to say
In my death-hour, except to her and thee!
Farewell unto thee, Halban; she will know it.
Throw down the kerchief if to-morrow morn—
But what is that? Dost hear? There comes a knocking.”
[pg 90]
“Who goeth there?” three times the sentry cried.
“Woe!” answered many voices wild and strange.
Resistance none the sentry might oppose;
The door could not withstand the heavy shocks.
The invaders passed the lower galleries through,
And mounted up the winding iron stair
That led to Wallenrod’s last dwelling-place.
Alf with the iron bolt secured the door,
His sabre drew, a cup raised from the board,
Drew near the window. “It is done!” he cried.
He filled, and drank. “Old man, ’tis in thy hands.”
Halban grew pale. With motion of his hand

He thought to spill the draught—he stopt in thought.

The sounds aye nearer through the doors were heard,

His hand relaxed. "'Tis they, the foes are come!"

"Old man, thou knowest what this uproar means?

What are thy thoughts? Thou hast the goblet full—

I have drunk my portion. In thy hands, old man."

Halban gazed on in silence of despair.

"No, no, I will survive even thee, my son!

[pg 91]

I would as yet remain to close thine eyes,

And live, so that the glory of thy deed,

I to the world may tell, to ages show.

I'll traverse Litwa's castles, hamlets, towns;

And where I pass not, there my song shall fly.

The bard shall sing them unto knights in war,

And women sing them for their babes at home.

Aye! they shall sing them, and in future days

Some venger shall arise from out our bones."[25]

Alf fell upon the window-sill with tears,

And long, long time upon the tower he gazed,

As though he yet his gaze would satiate

With those dear sights he shortly must forego.

He hung on Halban's neck; they mixed their sighs,

In that embrace of long and last farewell.

But at the bolts they heard a steely rattle,

And armèd men came in, and called Alf s name.

"Traitor, thy head must fall beneath the sword;

Repent thee of thy sins, prepare for death!

Behold this old man, chaplain of the Order,

Cleanse thou thy soul and make a fitting end!”

[pg 92]

Alf stood with drawn sword ready for their coming;

But paler aye he grew, he bowed, and tottered,

Leaned on the sill; casting a haughty glance,

His mantle tore off, flung the Master’s badge

On earth, and trampled scornful under foot.

“Behold the sins committed in my life.

Ready am I to die; what will ye more?

The annals of my ruling will ye hear?

Look on these many thousands hurled to death,

On towns in ruins, and domains in flames.

Hear ye the storm-winds? clouds of snow drive on;

Thither your army’s remnants freeze in ice.

Hear ye? The hungry packs of dogs do howl,

They tear each other for the banquet’s remnant.

“I caused all this, and I am great and proud,

So many hydras’ heads one blow has felled;

As Samson, by once shaking of the column,

To o’er throw the temple, dying in its ruin.”

He spoke, looked on the window, and he fell.

But ere he fell, he cast the lamp to earth.

It three times glimmered with a circling blaze,

That rested latterly on Konrad’s brow;

[pg 93]

And in its scattered flow the fire’s rust gleamed,

But ever deeper into darkness sank.

At length, as though it gave the sign of death,

One last great ring of light shot forth its blaze;

And in this blaze were seen the eyes of Alf,

All white in death, and now the light was dark.

And at this moment through the tower walls pierced

A sudden cry,16 strong, lengthened, broken off—

From whose breast came it? Surely ye can guess

But he who heard it readily might tell,

That from the breast whence such a cry escaped,

Now never more should any voice come forth.

For this voice a whole life spoke aloud.

Thus lute strings, shuddering from a heavy stroke,

Vibrate and burst; in their confusèd sounds

They seem to voice the first notes of a song,

But of such song let none expect the end.

Such be my singing of Aldona's fate.

Let music's angel sing it through in heaven,

And thou, O tender reader, in thy soul.

---

[pg 95]

# NOTES.

*(1) "In towers of Marienbourg the bells are ringing."*

Marienbourg, in Polish Malborg, a fortified town, formerly the capital of the Teutonic Order, under Kazimir Jagellon (1444-1492) united to the Polish

Republic; later on, given as a pledge to the Margraves of Brandenburgh. It came at last into the possession of the Kings of Prussia. In the vaults of the castle were the graves of the Grand-Masters, some of which are still preserved.

(2) *"But foreign houses of his fame were full."*

Houses—so were called the convents, or rather castles, scattered through various parts of Europe.

(3) *"The strife of keen-edged swords" = combattre à outrance.*

(4) *The Archkomtur.*

The Grosskomthur was the chief officer after the Grand-Master.

(5) *"Some unknown pious woman from afar."*

The chronicles of that time speak of a country girl, who, having come to Marienbourg, asked to be walled up in a solitary cell, and there ended her life. Her grave was famous for miracles.

(6) *"Our master he."*

In time of election, if opinions were divided or uncertain, similar occurrences were often taken as omens, and influenced the decisions of the chapter. Thus Winrych Kniprode gained all the voices, because some of the brothers heard, as though from the tombs of the Grand-Masters, a three-fold calling: "Vinrice, ordo laborat."

(7) *"A fire eternal burns in Swentorog's halls."*

The castle of Wilna, where formerly was maintained the Znicz; that is, an ever-burning fire.

(8) *"The place was Witold's."*

[Witold, the son of Kiejstut, after rising over the heads of the other Lithuanian princes to the sovereignty of the whole country, was ultimately dispossessed by his cousin Jagellon, founder of the Jagellon dynasty, which reigned over Poland and Lithuania from 1386 to 1572.]

(9) *Song of the Wajdelote.*

The Wajdelotes, Sigonoci, Lingustoni were priests whose office was to relate or sing to the people the acts of their forefathers at all festivals. That the old Lithuanians and Prussians loved and cultivated poetry is proved by the enormous number of ancient songs, still remaining among the common people, and by the testimony of chroniclers. We read that during a grand festival on the occasion of the election of the Grand-Master Winrych von

Kniprode, a German Minnesinger, being honoured with applause and a gold cup, a Prussian named Rizelus, was so encouraged by this good reception of a poet, that he entreated for permission to sing in his native Lithuanian tongue, and celebrated the deeds of the first king of the Litwini, Wajdewut. The Grand-Master and the knights, not understanding and disliking the Lithuanian speech, ridiculed the poet, and gave him a present of a plate of empty nutshells. In Prussia the Crusaders forbade officials and all who approached the court to use the Lithuanian tongue, under penalty of death; they banished from the country, together with the Jews and gipsies, the Wajdelotes, or Lithuanian bards, who alone knew and could relate the national annals. Again in Lithuania, after the introduction of the Christian faith and the Polish language, the ancient priests and the native speech fell into disrepute, and were forgotten; thence the common people, changed to serfs, and attached to the soil, having abandoned the sword, also forgot those chivalric songs. Still something has remained of their ancient annals and heroic verse, long joined with superstition, communicated in secret to the people. Simon Grunau, in the sixteenth century, came by accident on the Prussians at a solemnity, and with difficulty saved his life, on promising the peasants, that he never would reveal to any one what he should see or hear; then, after performing sacrifice, an old Wajdelote began to sing the deeds of the ancient Lithuanian heroes, mingling therewith prayers and moral instructions. Grunau, [pg 97] who well understood Lithuanian, confesses that he never expected to hear anything similar from the lips of a Lithuanian, such was the beauty of the theme and the phraseology.

*(10) "Stands visibly the pestilential maid."*

The common people in Lithuania figure pestilential air under the form of a maiden, whose appearance, here described according to the popular song, precedes a terrible sickness. I quote, in substance at least, a ballad I once heard in Lithuania: —"In a village appeared the maiden of the pestilence; and, after her custom, thrusting her hand through door or window, and waving a red cloth, scattered death through the houses. The inhabitants shut themselves up in a state of siege, but hunger and other necessities soon obliged them to neglect such means of safety; all therefore awaited death. A certain gentleman, although well provided with victuals, and able to maintain a long while this strange siege, yet resolved to sacrifice himself for the good of his neighbours, took a sabre of the time of the Sigismonds, on which was the name of Jesus and the name of Mary, and thus armed, opened the window of the house. The gentleman, with one stroke, cut off the spectre's hand, and got possession of the handkerchief. It is true he died, and all his family died; but from that time the disease was never known in the village." This handkerchief was said to be preserved in the church, I do not recollect of what village. In the East, before the appearance of the plague, a phantom with bats' wings is said to appear, and to point with its fingers at those condemned to die. It appears as though popular imagination wished to present, by such images, that mysterious foreboding and strange anxiety which usually precedes great misfortune or destruction, and which often is shared, not by individuals only, but by whole nations. Thus in Greece were forebodings of the long duration and terrible results of the Peloponnesian war; in the Roman Empire of the fall of monarchy; in America of the coming of the Spaniards.

*(11) "The trees of Bialowiez."*

[The trees here referred to are of an immense age and extra-ordinary height, challenging comparison with the giant trees of California. Many of them were venerated as divinities by the pagans of Lithuania, in whose religion tree and serpent worship formed a prominent feature. Oracles were supposed to be given from a peculiar species of oak, called Baublis, ever green both summer and winter. In the trunk of one of these, cut down about the year 1845, there were counted 1417 rings.]

[pg 98]

*(12) "Do burn the German knights in sacrifice."*

The Lithuanians used to burn prisoners of war, especially Germans, as offerings to the gods. For this purpose was set aside the leader, or the most distinguished of the knights for high descent and bravery; if several had become prisoners, the unfortunate victim was chosen by lot. For example, after the victory of the Lithuanians over the Crusaders, in the year 1315, Stryjkowski says: "And Litwa and Zmudz (Samogitia) after this victory, and after taking abundant spoil from their conquered and thunder-stricken foes, when they had paid to their gods sacrifices and the accustomed prayers, burnt alive a distinguished Crusader of the name of Gerard Rudde, the chief of the prisoners, with the horse on which he made war, and with the armour which he had worn, on a lofty pile of wood; and with the smoke they sent his soul to heaven, and scattered his body to the winds with the ashes."

*(13) "They gave me the name of Walter."*

Walter von Stadion, a German knight, taken prisoner by the Lithuanians, married the daughter of Kiejstut, and with her secretly departed from Lithuania. It frequently occurred that Prussians and Lithuanians, carried off as children, and educated in Germany, returned to their country, and became the bitterest foes of the Germans. Thus the Prussian Herkus Monte was remarkable in the annals of the Order.

*(14) War.*

The picture of this war is drawn from history. [The circumstances of Napoleon's retreat from Moscow, no doubt largely furnished the painful and realistic details in the text.]

*(15) "The secret tribunal descends to council."*

In the Middle Ages, when powerful dukes and barons frequently permitted themselves great crimes, when the power of ordinary tribunals was too weak to humble them, secret brotherhoods were formed, whose members, unknown to one another, bound themselves by oath to punish the guilty, not pardoning even their own friends or relatives. As soon as the secret judges had pronounced the decree of death, the condemned man was made aware of it, by a voice calling under his windows, or somewhere in his presence, the word —*Weh!* (woe!) This word, three times repeated, was a warning that he who heard [pg 99] it should prepare for death, which he must infallibly and unexpectedly receive from an unknown hand. The secret court was called the *fehm* tribunal (Vehmgericht) or Westphalian. It is difficult to determine its origin; according to some writers it was instituted by Charlemagne. At first necessary, it gave opportunity for many abuses later on, and governments were forced to exercise severity occasionally against the judges themselves, before this institution was completely overthrown. [Scott's graphic description in "Anne of Geierstein" of the court and procedure of the Vehmgericht will be instantly suggested.]

*(16) "A sudden cry."*

—*"What cleaves the silent air,*

*So madly shrill, so passing wild?*

*It was a woman's shriek, and ne'er*

*In madlier ascents rose despair;*

*And they who heard it as it passed,*

*In mercy wished it were the last."*—PARISINA.

[The coincidence, or borrowing of ideas, is manifest, but the image has been amplified and beautified in the Polish poem.]

*N.B.*—In all the Polish words retained in the text, *j* is pronounced like *y*, and *w* like *v*.

Lightning Source UK Ltd.
Milton Keynes UK
UKHW012000270720
367273UK00005B/358